-Paul + James-
To all the
differences + similarities
that unite us!

♡ Zurokk Zulkahoyde

MY NAME IS ZEDONK

JIA HAN

PLUM BLOSSOM
BOOKS

Hi there!
I'm a ZEDONK.

My mama is a donkey.

My papa is a
zebra.

Grandma says although Mama
and Papa are alike in some ways,
they are also a bit different.

She also likes to say
that when Mama and
Papa saw each other
in the fields one day,

they fell in love

at first sight.

When Mama and Papa
were first together,
they were happy
in the day . . .

and happy in the night.

They each had one concern, however.

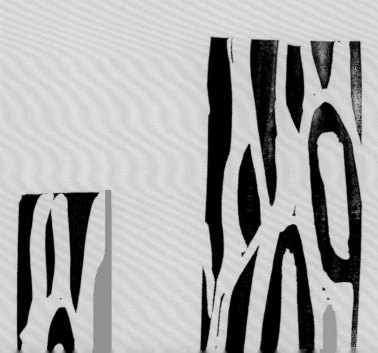

Mama is a
donkey,

while Papa is a zebra.

Usually donkeys
only live with
other donkeys

and zebras
with other
zebras.

Mama wondered how they might live together.

So Mama, without telling Papa, disguised herself as a zebra.

And Papa, without telling Mama, disguised himself as a donkey.

Then they looked for each other
here, there, and everywhere.
Mama and Papa wandered about
all day and finally met each
other on their way home.

When they saw each other in their disguises, they laughed and laughed for a long time.

They knew they loved
each other
just as they were.

Soon after,
Mama and Papa got married
and I was born!

I'm a
ZEDONK,
and my name is also
ZEDONK.
I like to run freely
in the fields.

I have many friends.

My mama is a donkey,

my papa is a zebra,

and I am a ZEDONK.

Each of us is a bit different and
we are all happy together.

RELATED TITLES FROM PARALLAX PRESS

Plum Blossom Books, the
children's imprint of Parallax
Press, publishes books on
mindfulness for young people
and the grown-ups in their lives.

Parallax Press
P.O. Box 7355
Berkeley, CA 94707
parallax.org

FSC
www.fsc.org

MIX
Paper from
responsible sources
FSC® C005912